Even in the days of legalized abortion there are no easy answers for a young woman who may be pregnant. Mia is an intelligent high-school student living in a Stockholm suburb. Her parents are understanding, although they are too preoccupied with their own marital problems to be of help.

For four agonizing days Mia—who is waiting for the results of a pregnancy test—thinks about what she wants to do with her life, and whom to turn to. There is her grandmother, there is the school counselor, there is Jan himself.

Ultimately, Mia realizes that she must make her decision alone—and for herself.

Young men and women will find this an important book for its honesty and deep commitment to a morality as relevant today as it ever was.

GUNNEL BECKMAN lives in Solna, Sweden, with her husband. The mother of five children, she edited the women's page of a daily newspaper in Gothenberg and has worked as a probation officer. Ms. Beckman has written a number of books for young people, two of which have appeared in English, ADMISSION TO THE FEAST (available in a Laurel-Leaf edition) and A ROOM OF HIS OWN.

THE LAUREL-LEAF LIBRARY brings together under a single imprint outstanding works of fiction and nonfiction particularly suitable for young adult readers, both in and out of the classroom. The series is under the editorship of Charles F. Reasoner, Professor of Elementary Education, New York University.

Mia Alone

GUNNEL BECKMAN

translated from the Swedish
by Joan Tate

Published by
Dell Publishing Co., Inc.
1 Dag Hammarskjold Plaza
New York, New York 10017

Mia ran up the narrow emergency stairs, slamming down the heels of her boots, the echo ringing around the dirty yellow concrete stairwell.

She took the stairs two at a time, her shoulder bag hitting the wall with a dull thump at each stride. Suddenly her heel caught in her flared pants leg and she almost lost her balance. At the last moment she grabbed the iron railing and found herself on her knees. She stayed still for a moment, listening to the thumping of her heart and her breath rasping in her throat.

There was a smell of floor-cloth and wet stone. A revolting basement-like smell.

Then she started running again—one two three . . . run . . . run . . .

God, wasn't she at the top yet? Help, only the fifth floor. What a stupid idea to race up these awful stairs instead of taking the elevator like a normal person.

But she wasn't a normal person . . . one two three

. . . not normal . . . half crazy, really crazy . . . her
head ached . . . the taste of beer rose in her throat in
sour bubbles. God, suppose she was sick here on the
stairs. She threw herself down on the bottom step of
the sixth floor and remained there, her forehead
against the wall. At that moment the timed light went
out and she was left in the pitch dark, only the little
red eye of the switch glowing mockingly at her.

Mia didn't bother to get up and switch the light on
again. She stayed there, her head against the wall, en-
joying the pleasant coolness of the stone surface. The
blood throbbed in her cheeks and ears, but the nausea
slowly retreated.

In the still darkness, her thoughts came creeping
back, scratching at the door, those confused obstinate
threatening thoughts that she had deliberately kept in
the background almost all day, but which now rushed
in and enveloped her.

If she could get to the drugstore tomorrow . . .

If she then got the results?

If it was true?

If . . . if . . . if . . . that damned *if* had been
lying there like a lump of lead in her stomach for an
eternity now, spreading a kind of paralysis all through
her body and soul, a paralysis which stopped her from
thinking and feeling and doing anything sensible.

Talk to someone—Mother, the school counselor, Jan.

But suppose it was just a false alarm—all that fuss
for nothing. But of course she should have done something. Sensible people find out . . . don't just go
around like a sack of potatoes. There were even tests
you could do yourself.

At first she'd thought it was her usual irregularity.
That had happened often enough and eight or even

ten days had gone by sometimes. She simply couldn't *understand*; that it could happen just like that! And Jan had said it was so safe. What an idiot she'd been.

Later she'd thought it was the stress of her new school, nerves and all that, but then days had gone by, rushed by, flown by. Never had days been in such a hurry to accumulate into weeks.

It was only the last ten days that she'd been really worried. It was crazy she hadn't gone then . . . after twelve days.

But she didn't have any money. And could you get that on credit? If anything should be free, then that should. Even then it wasn't all that reliable. She'd read in the evening paper about people who'd had wrong reports, people who'd at first been overjoyed and then miserable, or vice versa.

Anyway, she couldn't go to the local drugstore. Dad's cousin Kerstin worked there. Not that she'd necessarily gossip—but you could never tell. She'd know.

She ought to talk to Mother about it.

She wouldn't be angry or anything like that. But upset, of course—and disappointed. They'd had all that out ages ago, lots of times. Mia, who was such a clever and sensible girl . . .

But Mother was always busy nowadays, her job in the daytime and then her evening classes. And she seemed so depressed. That had been going on for a long time. Dad, too.

It had begun early last spring—Mia had heard them quarreling through the bathroom wall sometimes, though she hadn't worried all that much about it then; she had worries enough of her own. And then summer had come and the new school. And then Jan.

It would really have been much better to go and

see some complete outsider at some advice bureau or something. Of course, she could go to the school counselor. That's just what they were there for; they were pledged to secrecy and all that and knew exactly what you should do. If she'd still been going to her old school, then perhaps she would have done that. Mrs. Lindberg had always been awfully nice. But this new one scared her, young and pretty and confident.

It'd be hard on Mother, too, running off to confide in a strange counselor. Mother and Dad would have to know about it sooner or later.

If there was anything to know about. God, how idiotic to flap about like this when it wasn't even certain yet. It wasn't certain at all!

Ann-Margaret at her old school had been really overdue last spring and then it'd come as usual—she said it was *psychological*—that your period didn't come just because you were so hellish afraid it wouldn't. Perhaps it was the same for her? But how long could that affect you? Not forever, surely . . . twenty-three days?

No, today was the twenty-fourth. Twenty-four.

Mia shivered and suddenly realized she was icy cold all down her back, and her neck was stiff. Laboriously, she got to her feet and switched on the light. She picked up her beret, which had fallen off, and her bag, which had slid down a couple of steps. The knees of her red corduroys were dirty and one glove had vanished.

But she couldn't be bothered to look for it. The hell with everything, she thought wearily and went on up the last flight of stairs, her feet dragging.

It was deafeningly quiet in the apartment as Mia tiptoed into the hall, but while she was hanging up her outdoor clothes she heard her mother's voice coming from the bedroom.

"Is that you, Arne?"

"No, Mother, it's me. Be with you in a minute."

Mia went over to the hall mirror and looked at her flushed shiny face under the black bangs.

"I look like a ghost," she mumbled, combing through her sticky hair with her fingers and wiping her nose.

"Did I wake you up?" she said, standing in the doorway.

"Oh, no," said her mother, blinking in the light. "I hadn't gone to sleep. I sat up late with some work I'd promised I'd do for the firm, and then I went to bed and did my homework." She nodded toward the bedside table, on which lay an English grammar book.

Mia remained where she was, absorbing the warmth from the room.

The bedside lamp's orange shade spread a friendly light, which made the roses on the nylon quilt glow. There was a faint smell of the perfume in Mother's cleansing cream, and the clock on the bedhead shelf was ticking quietly and slightly irregularly as usual. This bedroom was the only room that had been really just the same after the move. It felt nice and secure to see the old beds with their scratched paintwork, the enlarged wedding photograph by the dressing table . . . the poster about bull fighting from their trip to Spain . . . Dad's ancient bathrobe on a hook by the closet . . . the cross-stitched cushion Gran had sewn in the basket chair.

Everything appeared to be "nice and secure," and Mother was lying there looking pretty in her blue nightgown, her long fair hair plaited at the back of her neck. It could have been the right moment to throw yourself into her arms and tell her everything. Mia went across and sat down on the edge of the bed.

Then she saw the wet rolled-up handkerchief on the bedside rug. Mother had been crying again.

When Mia looked up, she saw that her mother's eyelids were swollen. So it wasn't the right moment. The warmth and security of the room was an illusion. A strange mixture of impatience, disappointment, and relief came over Mia; perhaps relief more than anything else, relief over once again being able to postpone it all, scuttle back into your corner and hide, pulling the blanket over your head, pretending that if you didn't say anything, it didn't exist.

"Did you have a good time?" she heard her mother ask, but she couldn't answer. To avoid having to say anything right away, she leaned down and began to unzip her boots.

"Well, did you have a good time?" Mother repeated.

"Oh . . . sort of . . . a lot of girls from Barbro's class whom I didn't know and lots of chit-chat and sandwiches and beer and potato chips and cream cake and tea. Actually, it was kind of awful for Agneta, Barbro's sister, you know—her baby was yelling all the time."

"But—why? Isn't Agneta married, with a home of her own?"

"Yes, she was—but her husband's run off with another girl and Agneta's there alone with the kid. And since she's in her last year at nursing school, her mother has to look after the baby . . . and he's got that three-month colic or whatever it is babies get, so he just screams all day and all night. The whole family's hysterical about it. And Barbro says she's thinking of moving in with *her* boyfriend, who's got his own flat, before she goes crazy."

"So that then she can go back home with yet another baby," mumbled her mother with a grimace. "Poor things—but how can Elsa look after Agneta's child? I thought she had a job at the Post Office."

"No, she's given it up. What else could they do? They couldn't put him in a day nursery when he's sick."

"No, no, of course not." Her mother lay silent for a moment. "What a rat trap we women always end up in," she exclaimed finally, and her voice was so bitter and aggressive that Mia looked up quickly.

"But it was such a sweet baby," she heard herself say, as if she wished to defend someone.

"Babies are always sweet—that's the worst thing about it." Mia's mother laughed a little in embarrassment, as if wishing to cover up her recent sharpness of tone. "Anyway," she went on in a different tone of voice, "how are things with you? You're looking very flushed and you've black rings under your eyes. You're not sick, are you?"

"Oh, it's nothing . . . a little too much beer and running home . . . my feet were freezing. It's cold again and it's very slippery."

"Well, you really mustn't go and get sick right before Christmas. It's complicated enough already."

"Yes, it's the first of December on Saturday," sighed Mia. "They've put up the decorations in the pedestrian mall down by the shopping center already. Did you remember to buy an Advent calendar for Lillan?"

"Yes, and I even bought two, one charity one and one of the kind covered with glitter that she's been raving about—glitter all over it, with silver Christmas elves and princesses feeding squirrels and . . ."

"Oh," said Mia suddenly, smiling, "how I remember my first one—that huge one Gran gave me with a castle and hares and deer and Snow White. Golly, that seems a hundred years ago . . ."

She stopped and sat in silence. The memory of the glitter was abruptly extinguished, like snuffing out a candle.

If only it hadn't been Christmas. If only it hadn't been Christmas.

Mia's mother lay there in silence too, looking straight ahead of her. The light from the lamp suddenly seemed false, the clock malicious and irritating. Mia shivered and thrust her hands up the sleeves of her sweater.

The silence hung between them like a curtain; a transparent but impenetrable curtain, which neither of them could summon up the energy to break through.

"No, I really must go to bed now—I'm awfully tired, actually. You won't forget I can sleep late tomorrow, will you, so don't wake me until eight."

"I can't think why Arne isn't back!" Mia's mother said, glancing at the clock.

"Where is he tonight?"

"At the adult center, I think . . . or a council meeting or something . . . or auditing accounts or bowling or . . ."

Mia got up hastily. "Well, good night, then . . . sleep well."

She picked up her boots and padded over to the door.

"Same to you."

Mia had just got into the hall when her mother called her back.

"Oh, Mia, I totally forgot. Jan called again this evening. He sounded a bit low—said he hadn't heard from you since he called last Monday."

"That's right."

"Why not, Mia? I told you it was important!"

"Oh, it's not your fault."

Her mother lay silent for a moment. "It's nothing to do with me, but is something wrong between you two?"

"I don't know."

Mia stood in the shadow just inside the door, leaning against the doorpost. She suddenly thought that she would burst from the need to talk to someone, to cry, to be comforted. Her heart raced, her mouth went dry, and she swallowed and swallowed. Hesitantly, she took a step into the room.

"You see, Mother . . ."

Just then they heard the elevator stop on the landing outside and a minute later a key was thrust into the lock.

"It's Dad at last," exclaimed Mia's mother.

Mia turned around and bolted.

"It'll be all right, you'll see," she heard her mother's encouraging voice behind her. "You can't always be on good terms."

Mia hastily closed her door and threw herself down on the bed without turning on the light. "You can't always be on good terms." Oh, God.

Through the door she heard her father's voice, shrill and irritable.

She undressed in the dark, opened the window a crack and crept into bed without either washing or brushing her teeth. She couldn't face the risk of meeting Dad in the bathroom. She couldn't even face thinking, especially about Jan. She couldn't even cry.

She lay like a stone between the cool sheets, breathing in the frosty night air that trickled in through the window.

For the first time in her life the lightning thought that it would be nice to be dead flashed through her mind.

Down there—seven floors down, the Christmas tree with its many colored lights swayed in the wind, and the clock of the concrete church squashed between Domus and the employment office tinnily struck twelve times through the clear air. It sounded like a distant music box above the sound of the traffic.

In some way, there must have been a scrap of consolation in the sound, for Mia at once fell deeply asleep, like an exhausted child.

Although she'd gone to bed so late, Mia was already awake when her mother padded out into the kitchen and put the coffee on at about seven. Otherwise, she usually slept on until someone, generally Lillan, horribly lively and cheerful, shook her awake. But things had been different lately.

Sundays and weekdays, late morning or not, she'd awaken long before she'd needed to, as if a subconscious alarm clock had gone off somewhere inside her, and before she'd even opened her eyes, her hand had automatically gone down to see if anything had happened during the night. In case her period had come.

This morning she had already long since established that nothing had happened during the night. She'd even switched on the lamp and inspected her nightgown and the sheet. Nothing.

Feeling nothing else but a kind of sleepy resignation, she crept down beneath the covers again and put out the light, lying quiet, sleep still humming in her body, struggling against that vague leaden anxiety, unable to decide what to do. And having decided, what should she do first?

It was crazy that she hadn't been to the druggist or gotten one of those things you saw advertised for doing the test yourself.

If only she could get into town. Then she could go straight to that advice bureau.

It was quite unnecessary to upset Mother if there was nothing to worry about.

And then Jan.

What was she to do about Jan? She couldn't just go on avoiding him like this.

It was crazy.

He couldn't know . . .

Anyhow, she had to find out if anything was up *before* she saw him again. She couldn't just pretend nothing was wrong.

But *if* it were a false alarm—how would he react then? Would he be angry? But it wasn't her fault, was it? He knew she couldn't use the pill. It was he who . . . who'd said it was perfectly safe. He must have lots of experience, she'd thought. He was twenty and would soon be a qualified engineer. He might have asked some time if . . . But it was at least ten days since they'd last met and then it was only . . .

She had no idea what he thought about it, about—abortion. And what did she think herself? How could she possibly think anything? She'd never given it a thought. She'd read a little about the new laws that had been proposed, of course. But not in relation to herself. *It couldn't happen to her.* But she remem-

bered what her mother had said when she and Dad
had been discussing the abortion laws.

"It's obvious that only the woman should decide
whether she's going to have children or not! Isn't her
life as important as that of an unborn baby's? It's only
men who think they should always decide for women."

"It's not as simple as that," Dad had replied.

And another time—several years ago—her mother
had said directly to her:

"Promise me something, Mia. Come to me when the
time arrives and I'll help you about contraceptives; so
that you don't do as I did and be forced to abandon
your education and all that."

"Didn't you actually want to have me then, Mom?"
Mia had asked.

Her mother had flushed a little and patted her
cheek.

"Of course I want you now, darling. And to tell you
the truth, I probably wanted you then, too, although
there was such a fearful fuss at home. Anyway, there
was no question of doing anything else in those days—
You know, abortion was something unheard of then,
which you weren't allowed except in very exceptional
circumstances."

"But Mats, who died? Didn't you want to have him
either? And Lillan? You wanted to have her, didn't
you?"

"Mia darling," her mother had said, hugging her, "I
wanted to have you all. All I'm trying to say is that
you must be careful, so that you get a qualification
before you start a family."

Mia remembered that conversation now almost
word for word. But just afterward she had remembered only one thing: that her mother hadn't really

wanted to have her. That had hurt. And now it was
her turn. Suddenly she was a woman who had to decide whether a child, which was perhaps already inside her, should be born.

She must decide. Who else could do that? She
would soon be eighteen and was strong and healthy.

Should Mother and Dad decide if she were to have
an abortion? Or a school counselor? Or a doctor?

But she must want to herself. She was almost
adult . . .

Lillan's shrill voice suddenly came through from the
kitchen.

"Ssh! Mia's asleep."

". . . I only just lifted one corner," Lillan's voice
went on, now lowered to a hiss. "I only wanted to look
and see if . . . if it was the usual baby Jesus or . . ."

"I thought it was meant to be a surprise," said her
mother.

"Yes, but," cried Lillan, "it *will* be a surprise. I'll
forget about it, don't you see . . . you know how quickly
I forget things."

"Ssh! Yes, I've noticed that."

"Why's *she* sleeping late, anyway? Why can't *I* sleep
late sometimes?"

Sleep late. Sleep late—pleasant soft words.

Before—that is, quite recently—ages and ages ago . . .
that is, twenty-four days ago, sleeping late had
been a great thing; that scrumptious half-asleep condition, when you curled up under the covers and rel-

ished the warmth of your bed and the thought of not
having to get up right away and rush to the bathroom; just lying listening to the chatter of the others'
voices, the clink of china, smelling the smell of coffee
and cocoa blending into a sweet enticing vapor which
crept through the crack in the door.

Now Mia just became anxious, lying awake in there
while the others thought she was asleep, twisting and
turning and needing to go to the bathroom. Today it
was worse than usual since she'd gone to bed without
washing or brushing her teeth. She felt sticky, her
head ached, and there was a nasty taste in her mouth.
If only Lillan would shut up for a second. She sounded
like a noisy parrot.

The smell of coffee was suddenly unbearable. She
must get up and go out. She felt as if she were going
to be sick. Without putting on her robe and slippers,
she darted out through the door and straight across
the kitchen toward the bathroom.

"What!" cried Lillan. "Is she *awake?* And we've
been sitting here as quiet as mice! What's the matter,
Mia?" she cried, running after her sister. "What's all
the hurry? Have you seen my Advent calendar?"

"I have to go," hissed Mia, locking the bathroom
door.

"Leave Mia alone, Lillan," said Mother, putting
two more slices of bread into the toaster.

"No one's in such a hurry that they can't even say
hello," muttered Lillan, beginning to pack her school
bag. Then she brightened.

"How super that it's a nice day, isn't it? Maybe we'll
be able to go skating in gym today! With our new
guy."

"What new guy?"

"A kind of coach, awfully nice and awfully hand-some, with his red beard! He's called Bruno . . . super name, isn't it?"

"Hurry up or you'll be late," said Dad as he came into the kitchen with the newspaper under his arm.

"Oh, Dad, it's winter outside, have you seen?"

"Your socks, Lillan. You've left your socks on the chair."

With her school bag and skates dangling around her, Lillan darted back into the kitchen, this time hopping on one leg.

"Dad, you haven't given me a kiss today," she cried, hopping over to her father, who was standing by the stove pouring himself a cup of coffee.

"For heaven's sake, stop hopping around," her mother said. "There's no time for kissing now . . . off you go."

"I'll throw one to you then—look, here it comes." Lillan waved her hand and her glove flew across the floor.

"*Lillan!*"

A moment later the front door slammed shut.

"Heavens, what vitality!"

Arne Järeberg sighed and sat down with his cup of coffee. His long face was pale, and his square glasses failed to hide the pouches under his eyes. Despite his neat checked suit and the handkerchief matching his shirt in the top pocket, and despite a fresh smell of shaving lotion, he looked tired and worried. His thin dark side hair had been carefully brushed across his bald head and the lack of hair on his head was com-pensated for by bushy sideburns.

"Just as well someone has some vitality," his wife said shortly, pouring out another cup. God, how I hate those sideburns, she thought. He looks like a silly old playboy.

Her husband raised his eyebrows and said nothing. He opened the newspaper and began reading as he mechanically chewed his toast, equally mechanically raising and lowering his cup of coffee.

The kitchen was just as silent now as it had been noisy and full of life a few minutes earlier; only the rustle of the newspaper, the clink of china. An artificial wounding silence lay like a straitjacket over the two people sitting at the table. Arne Järeberg chewed and rustled; his wife sat staring out through the huge picture window.

It would be another half hour before the sun rose, and all the night lights were still glittering in the retreating darkness. The sky was cloudless and soon a giant pale sun would emerge over the old school hill. They'd said on the news that it was going to be a fine sunny day with a few degrees of frost.

Arne lowered the newspaper a fraction, though not so far down that he could look his wife in the eyes.

"Aren't you going to work today?" he asked.

"I'm going to the dentist, so I've arranged for the morning off."

"Oh." The newspaper was raised again.

"Arne . . ."

"Mmm."

"Arne!"

"Yes . . ."

"Arne, put that damned paper down for a minute and look at me. I can't stand this . . ."

Then the bathroom lock clicked and Mia appeared, enveloped in her father's bathrobe. Her face shone pinkly, newly washed, and the broad eyeliner effectively hid all traces of fatigue.

"Hi!"

Mia brushed her father's lowered cheek with her lips.

"Aren't you in a hurry?"

"No, I'm free before break," mumbled Mia, going over to the stove to heat up her cocoa. "Though I forgot to tell you last night, Mother. The staff is having some conference or other. Great, isn't it? In this fine weather too."

In fact she'd decided to stay home all day. Out there in the bathroom behind the closed door, she'd decided to stay home today and think; think in peace and quiet.

No one would be back until five o'clock.

A whole long necessary day to be alone in and try to think. Making the decision alone was a relief.

"Well, I must be off now," her father said, handing over the newspaper. "I expect the car will be hard to start if it's been as cold as they say. I might not be back for supper . . . but I'll call, whatever happens."

"But you know I've got my class tonight," objected his wife, and Mia saw a quick flush spread up her face. "That's the fourth evening running you've been out."

"Can't Mia look after Lillan?"

Before either of them had time to reply, he had smiled into thin air and vanished.

Mia turned quickly to her mother, who was sitting quite still, staring at the door.

"I'd better go." Mia's mother rose slowly from her chair. She brushed her hand across her face as if she were trying to control her features. The telephone rang.

"Järeberg here. Yes. Hello, Gran.

"No, nothing much. I'm just off to the dentist. How are you?

"Oh, dear. Have you asked the nurse about it?

"Yes, that's true. It always gets worse when the weather changes.

"This evening? I'm afraid that'll be difficult. Arne said he'd probably be working overtime and I've got my class, you know. I don't dare miss that.

"Oh, yes, it's Astrid, your name day today. I'd forgotten. Oh, what a shame."

"I can go and see her this afternoon," Mia said quickly. She'd just remembered that there was a drugstore near the old people's home where her grandmother lived. "Tell her I'm coming."

"Hello, Gran, just a moment. Mia here says she'd love to come up for a while this afternoon and have some birthday cake.

"All right, we'll do that, then. She'll be along some time after four. No, of course it's no trouble. She'd love to."

"That was good of you, Mia," said her mother, putting down the receiver.

"I like going to Gran's," said Mia, getting up. It was true and yet she felt ashamed.

"Of course," said her mother hastily. "It's just that it's so hard to find the time. And all this name day business is so difficult to remember. Oh, heavens, is

that the time? I must run. Don't forget to buy some
flowers. Where's my bag, and I'll give you some
money."

Yes, money. Money for the druggist; she'd forgotten
that.

"Mother . . . there's something . . . that has to be
paid in advance. You couldn't possibly give me an advance on my December money, could you?"

"Oh, so Christmas secrets are beginning already, are
they?" said her mother, opening her wallet. "You've
already had one advance, haven't you? It's going to be
tough squaring your debts."

"I'm working in the florist's at Christmas, you know.
You're supposed to get lots of tips, they say, so I'll be
all right, I think. If I could have thirty kronor, that'd
be fine."

"All right, that's your affair, darling."

All right, that's your affair.

Mia thought about her mother's words as she stood by the window and watched her red coat vanishing down there among the bare bushes and deserted sandpits. It was still very windy. There were a lot of cold sparrows about and the great tits were sitting like balls of feathers in the branches of the trees around the block. Mrs. Carlsson in the apartment next door was airing the bedclothes to the strains of Mozart on the radio.

All right, that's your affair.

Wonder if she would have said that if she'd known what the money was going to be used for? Never.

And whose affair was it, for that matter? That was what she had to sort out. If she'd been younger, it would have been easier in some way. Then it would have been her parents who would have had to decide. But now, she was old enough to marry even though she wasn't officially an adult. Granny, her mother's mother, had married when she was eighteen.

But if you're married . . . or if you live with someone, then you've got someone to share the responsibility. Though of course Jan had some responsibility in this too. But how many men would accept it? She'd read about the ones who just skipped out, who just said brutally to the girl that she'd have to clear up the mess herself.

Would Jan say that? No, she didn't think so. He had such kind eyes. Kind brown eyes.

But then she didn't know all that much about him.

Jan Håkansson, just twenty, a tall thin guy with kind eyes. And a beard and fairly long hair. Light brown hair and his beard a little darker. Pretty quiet . . . perhaps a bit serious, but maybe you thought that because his father was a free church minister. Jan had gone to night school and trained to be some kind of engineer, electronic or radio or something. And liked playing handball . . . going out on Saturdays or sitting in the bar, having a few beers. She'd been there with him several times. Otherwise they usually went to the movies or to Svensson's. Or just went out for a walk, sometimes just around the small open space the council had grandly named the Central Park, which her father always called Miller's Hill, because that's what it'd always been called before. Sometimes they'd taken a bus and gone out into the country and walked in the forest. Jan knew a lot about birds, which Mia did too, as Grandpa had taught her about them in Halland in the summers.

Sometimes they'd gone to a handball match, which she thought boring, although Jan got very excited.

Twice Jan had been back for a meal at Mia's and

both her mother and father had said that they liked
him. And she'd slept with him five times in his studio
apartment in the old house behind the sports ground.

What did it mean to know a person? Well, she knew
she'd fallen very much in love with him from the first
moment, when they'd met in the confusion of someone's birthday party; when he'd just danced with her
and walked home with her and kissed her in the doorway.

The worst thing was that now she didn't know if
she knew him at all. All this worry had meant that she
mostly felt a kind of . . . not exactly hostility, but . . .
all her other feelings seemed to have become sub-
merged. Sometimes she was furiously angry with him,
although it was no more his fault than hers. Of course
he'd persuaded her. She'd never slept with a man before.

It had seemed so safe.

It was so exhausting, all of it.

Though she had decided to go to the drugstore today, anyway. Today and not tomorrow or the day
after.

Today.

That was something, anyway.

Still wearing Dad's old brown bathrobe, which smelled of White Horse and old tobacco, Mia walked around the apartment savoring her solitude. It was ages since she'd been absolutely alone at home.

The silence enveloped her in waves, filling all the corners as if it were actually a substance. The ticking of the alarm clock on the kitchen table clattered loudly through the whole apartment, making the silence even more silent.

Imagine. Having hours and hours to yourself in front of you on an ordinary weekday. Long cool hours with no rush or fuss or chat or stereo or homework or setting the table or cooking fumes or Lillan's friends pouring in, giggling and spilling fruit juice and talking about horses.

And Mother who mustn't be disturbed so that she could study.

And Dad sitting at the telephone all the time talk-

ing about regional plans and rising rents and outward-
looking community activity.

Strange about this solitude, which could be so
horrible, and occasionally so marvelous.

Mia went from one room to the next, taking a sand-
wich in the kitchen, shutting the window in the
bedroom, tripping over the rocking chair's rockers, absorbing the different smells—coffee, soap, tobacco
smoke, new paint.

There was still something uninhabited in the air everywhere, especially in the living room, where the fur-
niture was new and unfriendly, too. Their old furni-
ture had been insufficient for the new apartment.

Mother hadn't wanted to move at all. The old place
had been much more rural and she'd been born in the
country. But the house was to be torn down and there
was nothing they could do about it.

The council had offered her father this apartment
in a new high-rise close to the center and Dad had
been pleased. He'd thought it was ideal to live so cen-
trally now that he'd begun to get so many local assign-
ments. But Mother said that high-rises were inhuman
and that the rent was too high and that they didn't
really need five rooms—or four and a half, as they
called it, since Mia's little room wasn't really a room.

Lillan had been just as pleased as Dad, because she
would be that much nearer the riding school where
she spent every spare minute. She was always talking
about Alexander and Caesar and Godiva or whatever
their names were, as if they were her best friends. Mia
herself had been more undecided. She had been going
to change schools anyway, when she'd got into high
school.

Of course it was a little sad leaving your old home

where you'd lived since you were born, even if it had been shabby and kind of dark. But it had only been three stories high, so everyone had known everyone else and there had been a cluster of fir trees outside where you could go sledding in the winter. Before . . . now nearly all her contemporaries had gone. So Mia hadn't really had anything against moving, although of course she'd been influenced by her mother.

Mia didn't really understand why her mother had been so against the move. Things were much better and more comfortable for her now—elevator, terrace, refrigerator and pantry and a very modern stove and lots of built-in closets and a great laundry in the basement.

And the view—from the seventh floor. It was like living on the upper deck of an Atlantic liner.

You could stand and just float out into the sunset or count thousands of stars in the evenings, stars you'd seen only in the country before. Far away the lights from the radio antenna shone like a wreath of red eyes and on the horizon the neighboring suburb lay like a glittering conglomeration of jewels. It was beautiful all right, even if there was a lot of concrete everywhere.

Mia remembered the first confused evening in the new apartment, with packing cases everywhere, bundles of bedding, wood shavings, and piles of china. There hadn't been enough light bulbs, and Lillan and she had sat in the dusk looking out through the living room's huge plateglass windows.

It was a windy March evening, small ragged clouds flying past like little hairy gray dogs chasing each other between the rooftops. But around the square in the center the ads winked their red, green, and white

MIA ALONE   33

lights and the unfamiliar sound of the evening com-
muter traffic had roared like the waves outside
Granny and Grandpa's farm down in Halland.

Lillan was playing spaceship with an upside-down
cake pan on her head.

"Now we're flying toward the Pole star," she
shouted, pulling a number of invisible levers and
pointing at a large yellow five-pointed star on top of a
building soaring up on the left of their field of vision.

"Look, Mia . . . it says something. It says . . . it
says . . . what does it say? I can't read what it says."

And Mia had leaned forward and spelled out the
ad.

"D A T E M A," she read out slowly.

"The star's called Datema," crowed Lillan. "It
sounds like Tintin."

"We live under the shadow of Datema," her mother
had exclaimed when she'd seen the computer ad.
"Typical!"

Neither Mia nor Lillan had really understood what
she'd meant, but Mia had felt that it had been di-
rected as a kind of reproach to her father standing beside her.

"If you think it's more human to live in the shacks
with outside privies in which I grew up, then you're
wrong," her father had said curtly.

"I didn't mean that."

"What *did* you mean then? You who're always find-
ing fault with this apartment and destroying the
pleasure for the rest of us."

"Now I've got to the moon," interrupted Lillan, who
hadn't been listening very carefully to her parents'
conversation. "And I want some food. You get awfully
hungry traveling in a rocket."

But Mia had gone into the empty little room along-side the kitchen which was to be hers and had sat down on her suitcase and cried.

It was the first time she'd realized that something was happening between her mother and father, that they were becoming unhappy with each other. Perhaps it had been going on for a long time, but she hadn't understood.

That's what was so horrible about growing older.

Things weren't the way you'd thought they were.

Mia took an apple and curled up in the corner of the sofa.

Anxiety had begun to gnaw at her again and she felt an uneasy sense of nausea. It must be imagination; you don't feel sick this early, she knew that. For the umpteenth time, she took the encyclopedia out of the bookcase behind the sofa and looked up *Pregnancy*.

Pregnancy, the condition in which a woman finds herself when she is carrying within her a fertilized ovum. . . .

The normal length of pregnancy is approximately forty weeks or 280 days or ten months of four weeks of what are known as pregnancy months. The approximate time of the end of pregnancy or beginning of delivery is usually calculated by counting from the first day of the last menstruation period one year ahead in time, then subtracting three months and adding seven days. . . .

The ovum and the fetus within it grows extremely swiftly (see Fetus). By the end of the fourth month, the fetus is already the size of a man's head and has grown up into the abdominal cavity from the pelvis. . . .

Mia snapped the book shut. She knew all that, didn't she? Yes, knew, knew, knew . . . that's what was so confusing.

All that you know and yet don't know.

You know lots of things but you don't understand them until you're involved yourself. Like when you're sitting looking around in the doctor's waiting room, and suddenly discovering that suffering and illness are right there beside you.

All that stuff about how a baby comes she'd known since she was five. It was a good thing to know, but not all that interesting in the long run. Then you got sex education at different stages at school and then it was quite exciting and a bit boring and some of it revolting, all that about ovaries and sperm and venereal diseases and contraceptives and that kind of thing.

It never seemed to have anything to do with yourself, really, although you understood perfectly well it was important. She'd been given a little book once, called—yes, what was it called?—*Sexual Love,* wasn't it?—but it had got lost.

You thought . . . oh, yes, I know all that—everything will work out all right. What should you do anyway? You couldn't very well go around swallowing pills for years just because some guy who wanted to sleep with you might appear on the horizon. Actually you were probably more interested in having someone to hold your hand at the movies. At least she was.

Of course there were others who were awfully ad-

vanced—at least it sounded so from all their talk.
Maybe she was a little backward. But in that case,
there were lots of others who were like that—girls as
well as boys. Just think of Bosse, whom she'd gone
around with for a while last summer—he had been
overjoyed at not having to do anything.

But you had that business hanging over you all the
time—that it was so necessary and natural and important and marvelously wonderful to go to bed with
someone as soon as you could; that you had to feel
backward or a failure or wrong in some way if you
didn't; that you were awful and lousy and hopeless if
you didn't want to. She hadn't really wanted to . . .
but Jan . . . though she *was* in love with him. It hadn't
been long before . . .

It hadn't been because she was afraid of getting
pregnant. It was mostly because she'd liked things as
they were. They'd got on well together without it,
she'd thought.

Of course things shouldn't be as they were in the
old days—lots of sanctimoniousness and sin and shame
and nice girls should keep themselves pure and the
others could go to hell or be ever so grateful that any-
one wanted to marry them.

Of course it couldn't be wrong to go to bed with
someone you're fond of.

But then you should also be able to be certain that
you didn't start a baby you didn't want.

They say it's all so simple these days. Freedom and
education and advice and contraceptives and almost
abortion on demand and . . .

And yet.

And yet there only needs to be a little hole in a
rubber sheath or some other slip-up for you to fall

into the same old rat trap, as Mother had said. Then finally chaining yourself to some unwilling guy whom you'd perhaps stopped being in love with long ago, who perhaps left you at the first possible opportunity, like Agneta's husband. And they were actually married.

Or becoming a Single Parent and seeing to everything yourself and abandoning your education and trying to get a job and putting the kid into a day nursery.

Or letting your mother look after the whole thing, and perhaps letting *her* sacrifice her job and her sleep and her energy.

Equally hopeless, all of them.

If you didn't choose—abortion.

Naturally that's the only sensible thing to do if you don't want to have a child at that particular moment. But how sensible are you?

And it's horrible to read about those long lines and that women with cancer of the womb perhaps don't get treatment in time because there are so many abortion cases.

That's crazy.

But what should you do, then?

Of course, an absolutely reliable contraceptive is the only answer. Lots of girls had been frightened out of their wits by the pill for a long time, though that was in the past now, according to the papers. But if your period is irregular, they won't give you the pill. Mia had asked the school doctor herself some time last year. And the new coil hadn't really come in everywhere yet.

But even if you find the best protection in the world, then of course there are always lots of people

who are just careless, or drunk, or else they don't care
what happens. Or something goes wrong. Or you
think nothing'll happen.

You simply can't grasp it. That a person comes into
existence by sheer chance; that you can get pregnant
so damned quickly. If there'd been abortion on re-
quest when Mother had got pregnant for the first
time, then Mia would never have had a life to live.
Quite a thought, wasn't it? Though it was horrible to
think like that. She wouldn't have been harmed by not
being born, and Mother would never have been able
to miss her.

But Mother's life had of course become different; in
what way, you didn't really know. Would she have
been happier? No one would ever know. How could
you know what was right? Was there any right or
wrong? It was probably as Mother had said that time,
that a woman must decide for herself if she wants or
doesn't want to have a child at a given moment.

But of course it's easier when you're grown up and
mature and know what you're doing and know that
you can't afford it or can't leave your job or whatever.
But—wasn't it just all those careless immature girls
who really shouldn't have children? And her? She
seemed to be halfway between the two.

Last night she'd dreamed about a child.

It wasn't Agneta's baby—it didn't have a face—it
was just there in her arms, holding on hard to her fin-

ger with its tiny hand, smelling delicious, like rose
petals.

The worst of it was that babies are always so sweet,
Mother had said.

And Mia suddenly remembered Aunt Eva when
she'd been visiting them and was looking at Lillan just
after she was born. "Quick—take her away—she's in-
fectious!" she'd cried. And yet Aunt Eva had four children already.

Mia knew what she meant now. She'd felt it yester-
day at Barbro's house, when she'd stood there with
the baby boy in her arms and he'd turned his head
toward her breast and sought after her with his
mouth. That longing beyond all reason.

And all that stuff you read about. The child became the love of my life and all that. Tough girls and
famous actresses who stepped forward and said that
children were the most wonderful thing that had ever
happened to them. And poor Fabiola and poor So-
raya . . .

Mia also remembered how she'd sat with some
other girls in their classroom, discussing what they'd
do if they'd just heard that they only had one more
year to live. Lena had said at once: "I'd have a child.
Not just because something of me would live after I'd
died, but . . . but then I'd have used my body for
something . . . absolutely . . . something important."
Someone had objected that there were more important things to do for the world than give birth to
one more child, but Lena had just replied: "Possibly,
but that's what I feel." And nearly all the others had
agreed with her.

God, what a mess.

But a person can't just be allowed to exist because

all . . . just because all girls dream of being mothers. Or nearly all.

Then it would also be wrong to use contraceptives. Like it was before, when it was a sin against God to stop a person's being born. Granny had told her about an old servant they'd had when she was little who'd had lots and lots of children. When Granny's mother had said something about not having to have children every year, she had replied, "But, missus, how will I be able to stand before Our Lord at the Last Judgment? Suppose he points at a row of small souls and says, 'You should have given birth to those on earth, Alida, and you didn't.' "

She hadn't given that old story a thought for ages and ages. Now a whole lot of things were coming to the surface of her mind just to confuse her.

But even ministers approved of contraceptives nowadays, and when the whole world was overcrowded with children, there must always be someone to care for. Why wasn't there an advice bureau for this kind of thing here and not just in the very center of Stockholm?

It was a *stranger* you wanted to talk to, wasn't it? Someone outside the family, a person you had no emotional ties with or whom you needn't shame or sadden. Someone you didn't have to meet again—as you would the school counselor. Every time you met her in the hall, you'd know that she knew that that girl . . .

Mia shuddered.

No, she'd go and have a bath now, a long hot bath.

As the the water was rushing into the bath, the telephone rang. It rang twice, three, four, and five times, but Mia didn't hear it.

When Mia finally staggered out of the bathroom, she was dizzy and her whole body was throbbing with heat. She threw her robe on the bed and walked around naked, her face flushed and her newly washed hair hanging in wet waves down her neck. She stood in front of the mirror to put her hair up into a roll on her head. When she'd done that, she stood there for a while, looking at her body from top to toe

She couldn't see that it had changed—the same narrow shoulders and small breasts, the same slim waist and broad hips and too big bottom. You didn't become Miss Sweden with that figure, but that had never really worried Mia much.

She held her hands over her breasts, which felt soft and warm, almost wet after all that hot water, her nipples spread out into large circular islands. But they weren't any bigger, were they? Or tender? And her stomach? It was just as small and flat as before.

"Three weeks," she mumbled, remembering that

picture of a three-week-old fetus in the encyclopedia.
It had looked horrid, like a little animal with a tail, a
seahorse or something.

*By the end of the fourth month, the fetus is already
the size of a man's head. . . .*

A man's head, for heaven's sake. She cupped her
hands over her navel. Then she snatched up her
candy-striped nightgown, pulled it on, and stuffed a
pillow over her stomach.

Oh, God, was that what you'd look like?

When she stood in profile, clasping her hands under
the pillow, she looked exactly like that picture she'd
seen in a magazine of the Women's Lib woman in the
United States who'd said to hell with the father of the
child and as a point of honor was going to be the only
light in her child's life. It had sounded from the article
that the child was going to have a rather rough time.

Exhaustion after the hot bath overcame her again,
so she threw down the pillow and crept into her un-
made bed, feeling like a large warm bun rising before
baking, swelling up larger and larger.

She closed her eyes and listened to her heart, which
was still beating abnormally fast, stretched her hand
tentatively out to the little transistor Jan had given
her, and switched it on.

*Whoever you are—welcome to the world—whoever
you are—welcome to life,* warbled Lill-Babs lustily out
of the radio and Mia switched it off again. She hadn't
the energy to listen to how Lill-Babs was urging her
on to follow that unknown child on its journey and
something else which rhymed with life.

Sleepily she began to leaf through an old weekly
magazine which had been lying on the bedhead shelf.
It was full of the Christmas joy to come: